To Maddy, Buzz, Dottie, and all living things as sweet in the world
—S. H. & S. I.

For friends, for family, and especially for love
—R. T.

SIMON & SCHUSTER BOOKS FOR YOUNG READERS
An imprint of Simon & Schuster Children's Publishing Division
1230 Avenue of the Americas, New York, New York 10020
Copyright © 2018 by Sean Hayes and Scott Icenogle
SIMON & SCHUSTER BOOKS FOR YOUNG READERS is a trademark of Simon & Schuster, Inc.
For information about special discounts for bulk purchases, please contact Simon & Schuster Special Sales
at 1-866-506-1949 or business@simonandschuster.com.
The Simon & Schuster Speakers Bureau can bring authors to your live event. For more information or to book an event,
contact the Simon & Schuster Speakers Bureau at 1-866-248-3049 or visit our website at www.simonspeakers.com.
Book design by Laurent Linn
The text for this book was set in ArrusBT Std.
The illustrations for this book were hand drawn, then textured and colored using Adobe Photoshop.
Manufactured in China
0918 SCP
4 6 8 10 9 7 5 3
Library of Congress Cataloging-in-Publication Data
Names: Hayes, Sean, 1970– author. | Icenogle, Scott, author. | Thompson, Robin (Illustrator), illustrator.
Title: Plum / Sean Hayes, Scott Icenogle ; illustrated by Robin Thompson.
Description: First edition. | New York : Simon & Schuster Books for Young Readers, [2018] |
Summary: While trying to save Christmas for her fellow orphans,
lonely Plum is magically transported to the Land of Sweets, where her pure heart saves the day for
King Christopher, King Patrick, and their subjects.
Identifiers: LCCN 2017061002 (print) | LCCN 2018006690 (ebook) |
ISBN 9781534404045 (hardcover) | ISBN 9781534404052 (eBook)
Subjects: | CYAC: Orphans—Fiction. | Loneliness—Fiction. | Magic—Fiction. | Christmas—Fiction. |
Kindness—Fiction. | Adoption—Fiction. | Kings, queens, rulers, etc.—Fiction.
Classification: LCC PZ7.1.H3967 (ebook) | LCC PZ7.1.H3967 Pl 2018 (print) | DDC [E]—dc23
LC record available at https://lccn.loc.gov/2017061002

Plum

Sean Hayes
&
Scott Icenogle

ILLUSTRATED BY
Robin Thompson

SIMON & SCHUSTER BOOKS FOR YOUNG READERS

New York   London   Toronto   Sydney   New Delhi

At Mary Fitzgerald Orphanage, Plum was often called the scrappiest, also the loneliest, but definitely the shortest.

"Plum is only as tall as my thumb!" Val would tease.

And the rest of the children would always laugh.

Plum dreamed of a family to love, who would love her back.
Wishing and waiting can sometimes feel lonely, but she
wouldn't stay glum. A bit of parchment, a few pieces of string,
some old fabric, and . . . *voila!*

"I'll call you Dottie," Plum said. "My best friend!"

"Your *only* friend," snickered Val

The adventure that truly changed Plum's life began on
Christmas Eve. The children were decorating the tree while
waiting for the post office to bring presents donated by the town.
But there was a terrible blizzard.

"Can anything be delivered in all this snow?"
Director Grittle worried.

"Not unless it's a shovel," said Plum.

With heavy hearts, the children finished
trimming the tree. There'd be no presents.
Plum had to find a way to help.

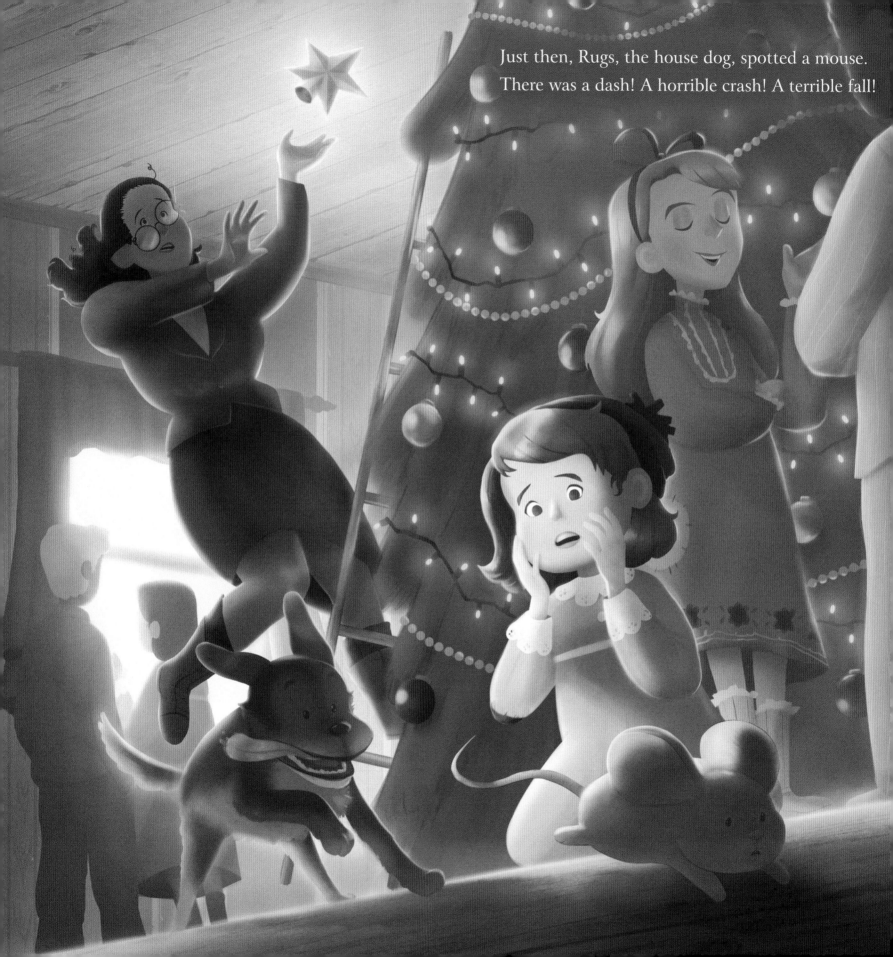

Just then, Rugs, the house dog, spotted a mouse.
There was a dash! A horrible crash! A terrible fall!

"How awful what clumsy Plumsy just did!" Val pointed.

All eyes turned to Plum. She knew it was wrong to tell a lie, but she also knew it was far worse to get a good dog in trouble—especially at Christmas.

"It's my fault," she said, and she bowed her head.

"I'm the one to send to bed."

Truthfully, Plum was glad to have the time alone. How else could she think up a plan to save Christmas morning? The children needed presents, and Dottie had given Plum the perfect idea.

She worked for hours and hours, and when she was finally finished,
Plum put her gifts under all the kids' pillows . . . even Val's.

When she returned to bed, Plum closed her eyes and whispered
the wish she wished every year:
  "Oh, Christmas stars on Christmas trees, guide us to our families."
  All of a sudden, there was a scatter and a scuffle below. . . .

With Dottie in her hands, Plum tiptoed down the stairs.
There was Mr. Drosselmeyer, a mysterious magician, who, on occasion, came to the orphanage to do amazing tricks. He gave a quick wink before slipping away. He left a small something behind.

"Look, Dottie," she whispered. "My very own present. But what could it be?"

Plum carefully examined the tiny package, a sweet scent filling her nose.

The Nuzzlecake inside was strange and sticky. Her stomach growling, Plum ate it up in one *gulp!*

Suddenly, the room started to twirl and swirl and Plum couldn't help but giggle.

The giggles turned into laughter, the laughter into hiccups, the hiccups into burps, and the burps grew into one big belch, and *poof* . . .

her ratty nightgown was transformed!
A magic pontoon filled the room!
Plum and Dottie climbed aboard and . . .

Whoosh!

They crashed through the front door and into a world made entirely of candy!

They raced through Fudget trees that had bark of glistening chocolate. They zipped past a row of Pollilops and made a sharp turn past the Twinkle Tarts.

"Even my dreams aren't this exciting!" she cheered.

The ride bounced to a stop beside two fairies who looked very dour.

"The Land of Sweets is turning sour!" Maritza explained.

"We can't even eat this Gummy Grass!" said Buzz.

"And things taste worse the closer you get to the castle."

"Maybe we can fix it," said Plum.

"Afraid not," said Buzz. "We're heading to the village to see if there are any sweets left."

"Then we better hurry," Plum said. "Hop on!"

Maritza and Buzz just stared at her, confused, not knowing what to do.

"See, the way it works is, we go to the village. The village doesn't come to us," Plum said with a wink.

They zipped through the Land of Sweets
until they came face-to-face with a giant
sugar dune.

"Let's get a move on!" said Plum.
They charged *UP, UP, UP* the hill . . .
until Buzz and Maritza took a spill!

"Help, help, help!" they cried.
The only way Plum could save her new
friends was to let her pontoon slide away.

"Thank you, Plum," said Maritza. "I thought we were done for."
"Now we'll never get to the village in time," Buzz added.
But Plum wouldn't stay glum. "Follow me!"

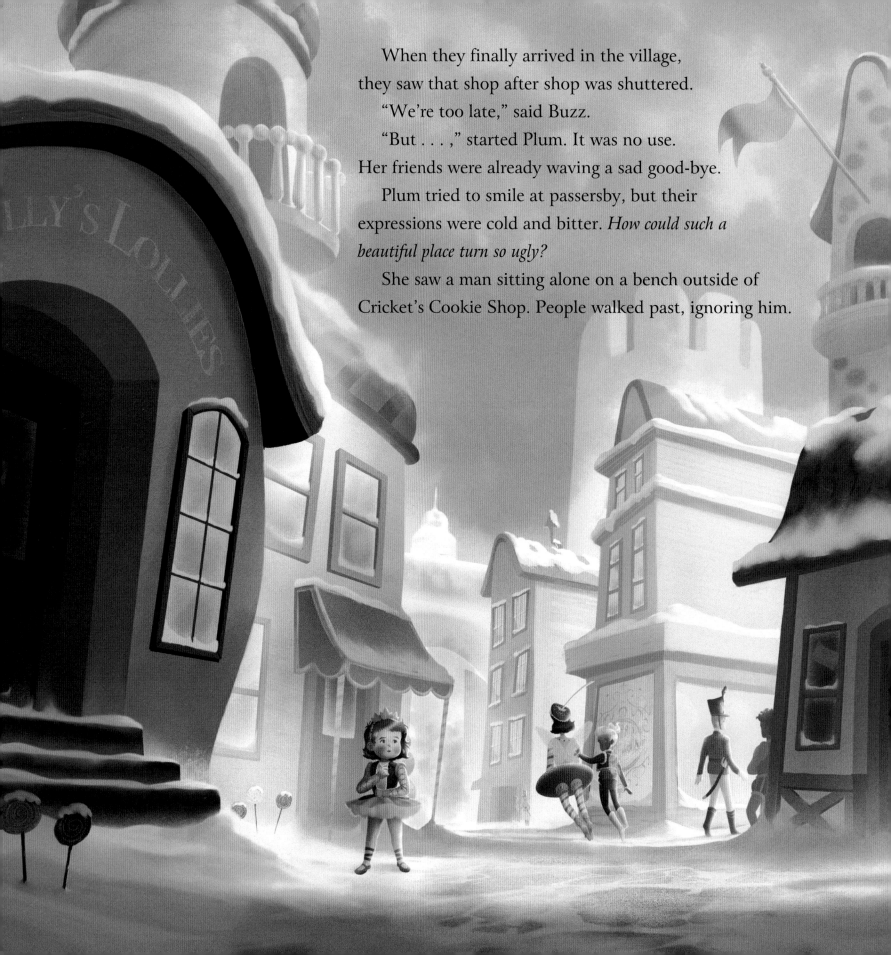

When they finally arrived in the village,
they saw that shop after shop was shuttered.

"We're too late," said Buzz.

"But . . . ," started Plum. It was no use.
Her friends were already waving a sad good-bye.

Plum tried to smile at passersby, but their
expressions were cold and bitter. *How could such a
beautiful place turn so ugly?*

She saw a man sitting alone on a bench outside of
Cricket's Cookie Shop. People walked past, ignoring him.

"I'm Plum," she said. "Is there anything I can do to help?"

The man didn't look up. "I'm afraid not, child. You see, our daughter was taken by the Lord above. It's been many years, but I'm afraid life has lost its sweetness."

Plum thought about all those Christmases at the orphanage, feeling so alone. All those years she wished for a family. . . .
And then she had an idea.

Plum held Dottie for the last time.

"Here," she said. "This is my best friend from the orphanage. She doesn't say much, but she has a lot of love to give."

The man was surprised. "If you have no family, how come you're giving her to me?"

"No one deserves to be lonely at Christmas."

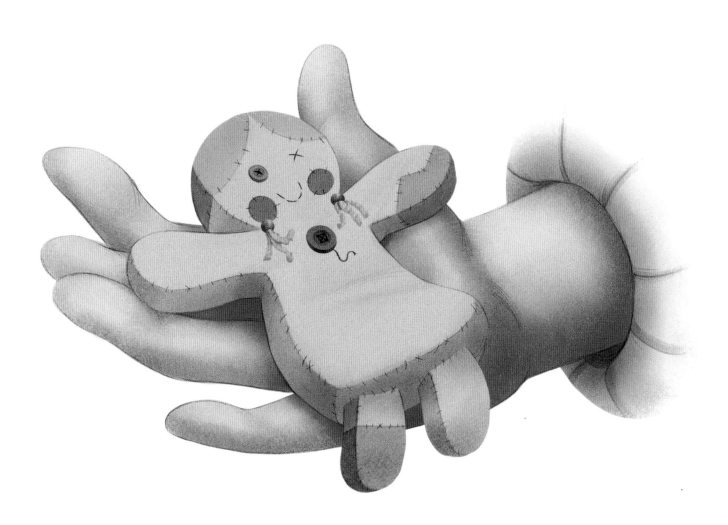

The man smiled. "Thank you, Plum. You are as sweet as sugar. Do you know who I am?"

"I just got here. I don't know who *anybody* is."

"I am King Christopher of the Land of Sweets." He then asked, "How would you like to be a part of my family? King Patrick and I miss having a daughter in our lives."

Plum's eyes filled with happy tears.

Just then, an older fairy burst out of Constanza's Confections, shouting, "I've just tasted the Pollilops and they're amazing! The Twinkle Tarts too! I can't believe it!"

Almost at once, the cloudy, gray sky began to brighten. The people of the Land of Sweets looked up and around and beamed! King Christopher and Plum raced to the castle to share their news with King Patrick.

Later, in the square outside the castle, King Christopher bellowed, "Plum has been proven to have the purest of hearts. And we have adopted her as our daughter!"

Plum and the two kings hugged once more, this time as a family!

They hugged so tightly that Plum started to giggle. The giggles turned into laughter, the laughter into hiccups, the hiccups into burps, and the burps grew into one big belch, and *poof*

Plum sprouted sparkling wings on her back!
They fluttered to life, lifting Plum straight up. The
people cheered as she flew through the air in huge circles.

Maritza pointed to Plum. "Look, she's a fairy just like us!"

And from that moment on, Plum was known across the land as
the *Sugar Plum Fairy*, the magical girl who saved their kingdom from
going sour with her sweet heart.

That night, after being tucked in by her fathers, the Sugar Plum
Fairy had one final, blissful thought: She felt so much love that she
vowed to make sure every child who still lived at the Mary Fitzgerald
Orphanage wouldn't stay glum . . .

. . . even Val.